THE MAGIC ROUNDABOUT

Dougal to the Rescue

Based on the BBC television programmes

by Serge Danot

Story by JANE CARRUTH

ODHAMS BOOKS LIMITED, LONDON

5s.

Dougal is feeling so lazy today. There he is in bed, with his best blue pipe.

"Ah! What a wonderful life!" says Dougal, as he puffs at his blue pipe. "How soft my bed is! Just think, I have the whole day all to myself!"

But as Dougal lies on his nice soft bed dreaming about mountains and mountains of lovely crunchy sugar, he hears a voice. It is a voice he knows well. It is old Mr. MacHenry's voice.

"Help! Help!" Mr. MacHenry is calling. "You must come and help me, Dougal, old friend."

Poor Dougal! Just when he is having such a lovely rest! But, of course, he must see what his friend Mr. MacHenry wants.

"It's my tricy-bus," says Mr. MacHenry. "It won't go any more. It has broken down."

Mr. MacHenry is very upset. He is nearly crying.

Dougal gives a great big yawn. But he says, "Don't worry, Mr. MacHenry. I am a very good repair man. I can mend anything. Just leave it all to me."

Dougal looks at the engine which makes Mr. MacHenry's tricy-bus go very fast up and down the roads.

He says, "Hmm!" Then he says "Hmm!" again, because he cannot see anything wrong with the engine.

"I'll give you a little push," Dougal says at last. So Mr. MacHenry gets onto his tricy-bus, and Dougal puts his head down and pushes. Mr. MacHenry wobbles and wobbles as the tricy-bus goes forward a few inches!

When Dougal stops pushing, the tricy-bus stops going forward. Dougal is very hot and tired. It is a long time since he has sucked one of his sugar lumps.

"I can't make it go," Dougal tells Mr. MacHenry. "I am very, very sorry."

"Dear me!" says old Mr. MacHenry. "I was sure *you* could mend it, Dougal."

"It's not my day," says Dougal, and then he gives a big yawn. "Where are you off to, anyway?"

"I must find Dylan."

"You mean that guitar-playing Rabbit," says Dougal. "What is the matter with him?"

"He is not well," says Mr. MacHenry. "I can make him better, I expect."

"I'll try once more," says Dougal, and he begins to push. Nothing happens, until, what do you think?

Mr. MacHenry suddenly remembers to *switch on!* It happens to the best of tricy-bus riders! "I'm off!" he shouts. "Thank you, Dougal!" He doesn't tell Dougal that he has been *switched off* all the time. And Dougal follows him in case he breaks down again.

When they find Dylan they see at once that he is ill.

"It's my lumbago," says Dylan. "I'm so stiff I can't stand up straight. Help me, Mr. MacHenry."

"You must have lots of fresh young carrots," says Mr. MacHenry, "Dougal will get them for you."

"I won't!" says Dougal. "I'm very stiff too, and I need lots of big crunchy sugar lumps." But in the end he goes off to look for carrots for Dylan. When he finds them, he has to take them back to the Rabbit.

Dylan is very pleased. He eats two, and then he cries, "Why, I feel a new Rabbit already. Thank you, Dougal!"

"I'm off to bed," Dougal tells him. "Nobody would guess that this is my Day of Rest!" And off he goes.

But just as Dougal climbs into bed again, he hears a voice. It's a voice he knows well. It's Florence's voice.

"Dougal! Dougal! Where are you?" Florence is calling. "Do come quickly, Dougal."

Poor Dougal! He is *so* tired and sleepy. He tries not to hear the voice.

But Florence keeps on calling, "D-oo-gal, where are you? D-oo-gal! D-oo-gal! Please come!"

Dougal is simply furious. "Who do they think I am?" he asks himself. "Why can't they give a dog a bit of peace!"

Then he thinks, "I'll hide somewhere! I'll go *under* the bed instead of on top of it."

But, of course, Dougal wants to smoke his beautiful blue pipe, and it's not very easy to hide *and* smoke at the same time.

"I suppose I shall *have* to go and see what Florence wants," Dougal thinks at last. "What a life!"

"There you are!" says Florence, when she sees Dougal. "I thought you were never coming. I have a present for you from Mr. MacHenry. Do you want to see it?"

"Yes," says Dougal. "Is it sugar, Florence?"

"Of course not," says Florence. "I'll show you." And she opens the box. There, inside, is a tartan bow-tie with the words *Made in Scotland* on the back.

"What is it?" Dougal asks. "Can I eat it, Florence?"

"No," says Florence. "You wear it round your neck."

While Florence is telling Dougal about Mr. MacHenry wanting him to have a present, Dylan and Brian find the tie. "I say, old boy," says Brian, "what on earth is it? It looks like a big butterfly."

Dylan the Rabbit pretends he knows about butterflies. He says, "Yes, yes, it comes from a foreign country. I have seen them on my travels. We should take it to the Natural History Museum. We might get a reward."

"I saw it first," says Brian Snail. "Don't forget *that*, old boy!"

Just then Florence and Dougal come back. "What is all this about a big butterfly?" says Florence. "Really, Brian, you are a silly-billy. That's Dougal's new tartan bow-tie. He is going to wear it round his neck."

"Let me try it first," says Dylan. And he holds it up.

"Do I look smart?"

"Give it back to Dougal," says Florence. "If you don't, I'll tell Mr. MacHenry, and he won't come next time you are ill."

Dylan gives the bow-tie to Florence, and she puts it on Dougal. Then she gets a big mirror so that Dougal can see how smart he looks. Dougal stares at himself in the mirror. He is very pleased with what he sees!

Then Zebedee comes along and tells Dougal that Mr. MacHenry is going to give a lovely party.

"You are the guest of honour," says Zebedee, "because you helped to rescue Mr. MacHenry."

Dougal thinks he would much rather go to bed with his best blue pipe. But he is much too kind to say so. Instead, he says, "Thank you very much, Zebedee, for telling me about the party. I shall wear my new tartan bow-tie."

Everybody is very pleased except Brian Snail. He wishes that Dougal's bow-tie was a butterfly so that he could get a reward for finding it!

You can read about the Magic Roundabout adventures in "Playhour and TV Toyland".

© English text, Odhams Books Ltd., London, 1967
Phototypeset by Keyspools Ltd., Golborne, Lancs.
Reprinted Dec. 1967
Printed in Belgium.